Robbi

riding through the forest,

scooping up the field mice

and bopping them on the head.

Down came the Good Fairy and
she said, "Little Rabbit Foo Foo,
I don't like your attitude,
scooping up the field mice
and bopping them on the head.
I'm going to give you three
chances to change, and if you
don't, I'm going to turn you
into a goon."

Little Rabbit Foo Foo
riding through the forest,

scooping up the wriggly worms
and bopping them on the head.

Down came the Good Fairy

and she said, "Little Rabbit Foo Foo,
I don't like your attitude,
scooping up the wriggly worms
and bopping them on the head.
You've got two chances to change,
and if you don't, I'm going to
turn you into a goon."

Little Rabbit Foo Foo
riding through the forest,
scooping up the tigers
and bopping them on the head.

Down came the Good Fairy and
she said, "Little Rabbit Foo Foo,
I don't like your attitude,
scooping up the tigers
and bopping them on the head.

"You've got one chance left to change,
and if you don't, I'm going to
turn you into a goon."

For Geraldine, Joe, Naomi, Eddie, Laura and Isaac
M.R.

For Elaine, Charlotte and Nicola
A.R.

LITTLE SIMON

Simon & Schuster Building, Rockefeller Center
1230 Avenue of the Americas, New York, New York 10020
Text copyright © 1990 by Michael Rosen. Illustrations copyright © 1990 by Arthur
Robins. All rights reserved including the right of reproduction in whole or in part in
any form. LITTLE SIMON and colophon are trademarks of Simon & Schuster. Also
available in a SIMON & SCHUSTER BOOKS FOR YOUNG READERS hardcover edition.
Manufactured in Hong Kong   10   9   8   7   6   5   4   3   2   1
ISBN: 0-671-70968-2   ISBN 0-671-79604-6 (pbk)

Little
Rabbit Foo Foo

Retold by Michael Rosen
Illustrated by Arthur Robins

LITTLE SIMON
Published by Simon & Schuster
New York   London   Toronto   Sydney   Tokyo   Singapore

Little Rabbit Foo Foo

Little Rabbit Foo Foo
riding through the forest,
scooping up the goblins

and bopping them on the head.

Down came the Good Fairy and
she said, "Little Rabbit Foo Foo,
I don't like your attitude,
scooping up the goblins
and bopping them on the head.

"You've got no chances left, so I'm
going to turn you into a goon."

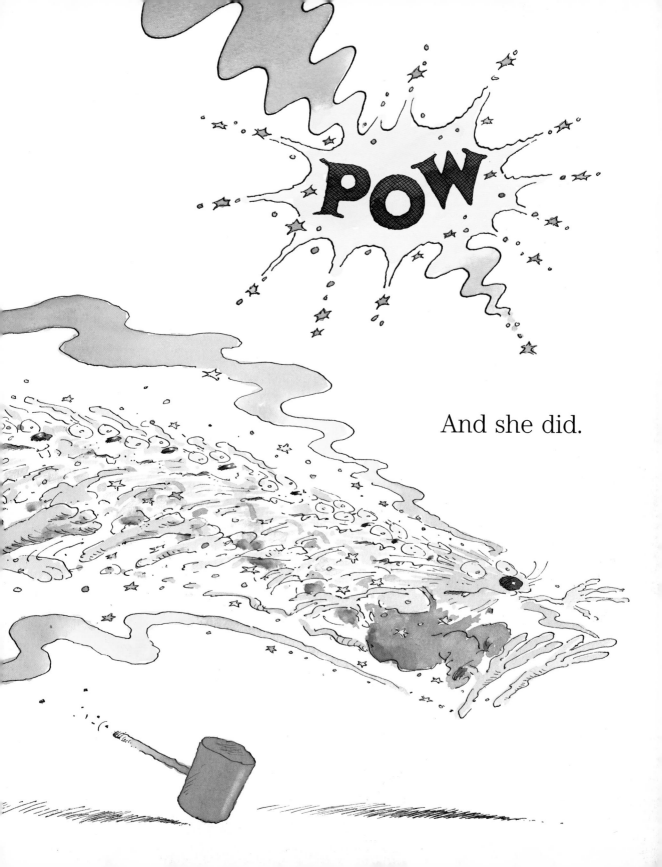

And she did.

The moral of the story:

Hare today,
goon tomorrow!

Little Rabbit Foo Foo

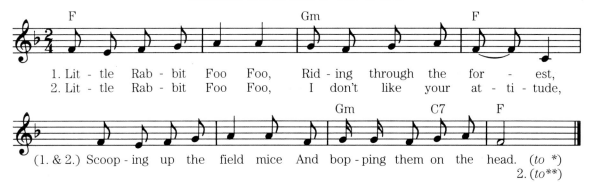

1. Lit - tle Rab - bit Foo Foo, Rid - ing through the for - est,
2. Lit - tle Rab - bit Foo Foo, I don't like your at - ti - tude,

(1. & 2.) Scoop - ing up the field mice And bop - ping them on the head. *(to *)*
2. *(to**)*

*(Spoken) Down came the Good Fairy,
And she said — (to 2.)

**(Spoken)"I'm going to give you three
chances to change,
And if you don't,
I'm going to turn you into a goon."

3. Little Rabbit Foo Foo,
Riding through the forest,
Scooping up the wriggly worms,
And bopping them on the head.

(Spoken) Down came the Good Fairy,
And she said —

4. Little Rabbit Foo Foo,
I don't like your attitude,
Scooping up the wriggly worms,
And bopping them on the head.

(Spoken) "You've got two chances to change,
And if you don't,
I'm going to turn you into a goon."

5. Little Rabbit Foo Foo,
Riding through the forest,
Scooping up the tigers,
And bopping them on the head.

(Spoken) Down came the Good Fairy,
And she said —

6. Little Rabbit Foo Foo,
I don't like your attitude,
Scooping up the tigers,
And bopping them on the head.

(Spoken) "You've got one chance left to change,
And if you don't,
I'm going to turn you into a goon."

7. Little Rabbit Foo Foo,
Riding through the forest,
Scooping up the goblins,
And bopping them on the head.

(Spoken) Down came the Good Fairy,
And she said —

8. Little Rabbit Foo Foo,
I don't like your attitude,
Scooping up the goblins,
And bopping them on the head.

(Spoken) You've got no chances left,
So I'm going to turn you into a goon!"
POW!!! And she did.

The moral of the story:

HARE TODAY, GOON TOMORROW!